MW01632944

JOLIET—a Novel

JOLIET—a Novel

Ray Vargo

VANTAGE PRESS
New York

FIRST EDITION

Published by Vantage Press, Inc.
516 West 34th Street, New York, New York 10001

Manufactured in the United States of America
ISBN: 0-533-10216-2

Library of Congress Catalog Card No.: 92-90694

0 9 8 7 6 5 4 3 2 1

Contents

Foreword

Lois and Clark—Rayburn and Finch—Joliet and Marquette—Nick Kenny.

The time frame? Autumn, 1954. The Midwest.

The signs ground into the dirt in a suburban cornfield going south on 66 out of Joliet are in eloquent reminder to a poetic frieze.

It gave MacDonald
that added charm.
Hello Hollywood
Goodbye Farm
Burma Shave!

A Riddle—

What was the product of a New York huckster's mind doing in that suburban cornfield at that altitude at that time?

If you comprende the answer you can proceed with this story because you have solved the riddle. The signs were just banged into the dirt with a hammer and you passed them every day and nobody paid any attention. *Que se dice en Italiano.* A riddle anyway.

The sun rises; the sun sets. The Earth revolves and people move from one location to another in a global frenzy for reasons they don't understand.

Sometimes strange and weird combinations of people come together in an imperfect world.

This story is just one small slice of that imperfect world.

—Royal Insurance Co.
New York, NY
October 1957

PART I

THE COMEBACK

The Texas Chief, out of Dearborn Street Station (7:00 P.M. CST), bound for the Deep South, snaked its way gracefully around a curve in the road, straightened out, hesitated momentarily, and then accelerated impatiently once again over the glazed sticks of track in central Illinois.

Snow had fallen heavily during the past week throughout the great Midwest, driving the temperatures considerably below freezing. It had finally stopped this last day of the year, backing off considerately, as if giving the year the option of going out and coming back in again clean. The wind that the snow had brought with it remained, however, to assault and whip you into numbness and sensibility if you happened to be impetuous enough to be caught outside.

The full, clear moon that was common on nights like this was right on top where it should be, highlighting the normally gray countryside, offsetting it, making it shine and glisten like a too-perfect drawing on the face of a Hallmark.

Inside the train, the passengers, especially the old ladies and young boys, still imbued with the holiday atmosphere Christmas had imposed, looked out at the passing scene wide-eyed and marvelled at the brightness, the solemnity, and the purity of it all.

For most of them, the men and the women, especially the women, as they glanced serenely across at their child or children, awake or already asleep just thirty minutes out of Chicago, it made them feel good to be alive and inspired thoughts of God.

The great common denominators, the night and the

snow, acting together in overlapped concert to cover the dirt and the grit and the nastiness of life. Why couldn't there be snow on the ground all the time and every night be New Year's Eve?

Occasionally their glances shifted from the scenery on the outside to center upon their fellow passengers. Most of them were going to at least Springfield or to St. Louis, and it was not unlikely or improbable that a friendship or two, however hastily evolved, especially on a night like this, would be made along the way.

The Midwestern element predominated in the half-filled coach. The old ladies going down to Dallas or Fort Worth to visit brother Elmer or cousin Nettie; the not-peculiar-to-anywhere, forever-present in-transit GI staring blankly out at the snow, confused, alone, detested, and ignored in most places outside his own camp simply because of his uniform (ironically, the one thing they told him at the recruiting station would be the badge of his manlihood and acceptance); the almost-childlike-looking young girl carefully cradling her own infant's head at the bend in her elbow at chowtime.

Occupying the third seat from the front of the coach, completely apart from the rest of the passengers and the across-the-aisle camaraderie that was in various states of development as the train rolled on, sat a very self-entranced young man. He wouldn't have had the time to hobnob with anybody even he wanted to, Not tonight.

Looking out the window, he saw the quarries at Lemont flash by blanketed in white as if being preserved for another, more propitious time of year. "Romeo Beach," he laughed to himself. "That was a hell of a place to swim. And I've seen better-looking broads light up on pinball machines. There it is, frozen solid. You'd have to be a damn polar bear to try it now."

Lemont . . .

Lockport . . .

Then Joliet.

The end of the line for you, buddy. It'd come up soon enough.

It was of growing concern to some in the coach that the young man put himself so obviously above everyone that it was impossible to pry him with direct looks. It seemed obvious enough to those who took note that from the cut of his clothes and his self-assured, almost contemptuous carriage he was an Easterner. New Yorker probably.

He was handsome and sharp-featured and aware of it and gave no sign of recognition to any of the people who smiled up at him as he showed some slight indecision while looking for a seat when he'd first boarded the train.

At first glance, with that boyish face and head-framed haircut it appeared that he might have been a college student home for the holidays. A closer, more carefully appraised examination, however, would have discerned the lines of wear and spent emotion around the eyes and in the forehead and promulgated the possibility of a successful junior executive.

His whole general air suggested a high degree of intelligence and professional remoteness; consequently, he couldn't be just anybody, and to a Midwesterner these things were important.

To the passengers, as they looked at him every now and then, he seemed to be lost in himself and completely unaware of any of their varying attentions. He just sat there gazing far horizontally out the window at the same general angle, not bothering to turn his head to give any passing thing a second look. It was as if he had seen it all before, been this way many times, and the whole thing bored him.

Lockport.

Coming into Lockport, buddy.

Lean forward just a little.

Take a good look.

Recognize it?

You should.

How many times had you leadfooted it through here at 3:00 A.M. on your way back from that worthless witches house in Orland Park that flashy "where've you been, let's for sin" bleached blond who used to wear the heavy cake makeup to hide the pits in her face?

Her and how many more like her?

Only no matter who it was or how much you put into it, it was always Joan's face you were facing, Joan's lips you were kissing, Joan's flesh you were caressing. . . . Only it wasn't Joan, and it made for madness and end-resulted you in the hospital after you tried to kill yourself.

Hey now!

Better snap out of it, Janik.

The hell with catching the reflection of those envious rubes behind you in the window.

You can study and amuse yourself with them anytime.

Better pay attention to where you are.

The next stop. That's us.

Everybody out!

Are we everybody?

Are we a genius?

Do we contain multitudes?

They said we did?

Horseshit!

Relax . . .

Lean back and relax, for Christ's sake. You're gettin' too damn edgy. You been this way how many times, and you still anticipate. When you gonna learn when you're dead?

Maybe you're more the rube than any one of them in the rear. Aren't even there and already you're beginning to feel yourself tighten up, right? It's beginning to hammer inside you, and your palms are beginning to get a bit moist, aren't they, buddy?

You jerk.

You classic jerk!

You twenty kinds of a horse's tail!

After all this time, you still haven't let up on it, have you, writer?

She still hits you as hard as she did that first Monday morning at OAC when you first laid eyes on her. Admit it!

Four blank, meaninglessly successful years, plus how many women and razed continents later, and this broad in this town whose name you never heard of until two weeks before you came here is the only thing you can look forward to and think of.

Brother!

You still look back and run it around in your mind and try to figure where it went wrong.

On the other hand what the hell difference did it make where it went wrong?

It's over. She's what she is and you're what you are and nothin' you got going for you is ever gonna change it.

Not ever.

You can reason and rationalize with all your acquired powers that she was only a flashy, classless, two-bit, small-town, Midwestern punk; reduce her point by point to nothing in your mind, as you've done so many times in the past, and only wind up the same way you always wind up: knowing that it's still there; that this one was the top of the hill and there'll never be anything else like her; that she was still the most beautiful woman you ever saw and no matter what mental contortions you go through in an attempt to shut her out, she's still got one helluva hold on you.

There's no prophylactic in this world thick enough against her. Liquor, other women, distance, or time.

You've tried them all in various shapes and quantities, but she eats through everything.

No point in kidding yourself, Janik. This'll be a dry trip like all the others before it. No sense to it. You lost all the illusions a long time ago. Even before you ever met her.

But it's New Year's Eve and a guy has to belong somewhere. And you're mentally down in Joliet all the time, whether you're physically down here or not, so you figure you might as well bridge the gap, bring the two together, sort of complete the circuit, in the hope that it will give you the same energy and spark that it did eternities ago when you first discovered yourself in her.

Not that you have any intention of putting it to any practical use of course. That and the sorry fact that it would be impossible to hit that peak and exact set of circumstances again. You've changed just as she's changed.

But just to be back and get the feeling of full-headedness and life-meaning that being here had given you when it was all new, that's all you wanted out of tonight.

Just a little truth and small-town realness to neutralize and cancel out the cheapness and big-time phoniness of the greatest city in the world. Maybe you could glean just that much from what was always here to be had.

Lost in the web of his own reasoning process, Janik was not acutely aware of the approximate second that the train began to brake down for its approach to the station.

The rest of the passengers, not used to the routine of the trip and eager for any break in the monotony, suddenly broke off their conversations with their neighbors and turned their squinting faces toward the windows. They were coming into a city. The first stop since they had left Chicago some forty-odd minutes ago.

The general, far-vista beauty of the snow-covered landscapes had suddenly been supplanted by objects that demanded close scrutiny and specific attention, as close and specific as you could possibly get on a moving train, even a slowed-down one.

On the right there were streets packed hard with a week's snow and houses with lonely electric candles burning steadily in the windows. There were lights embracingly arranged on various front porches and elaborate Christmas settings on floodlit front lawns.

There was the red neon AMERICAN STEEL AND WIRE sign coming up big out of the night on the left, prominently manifesting its meaning as unmistakably as the number of fingers suddenly thrust out of a tightly clenched fist.

On every side as the train eased forward, penetrating deeper and deeper, a city was beginning to cut her teeth and form her words. And to those who had never seen the city before or only passed through her occasionally in a car or on a train, the city said, "From where you see me, I am dirty and I am cheap. I am only the buildings and the sidewalks and the train station you will see in a very few minutes. Externally, as I appear, I am nothing special. You will see me and forget me under the weight of the next place the train stops. For you I have nothing."

To the slender, well-dressed young man casually slinging his topcoat over his shoulders, walking down the center aisle to the rear of the car, getting ready to detrain, the city had another message.

"I am dirty and I am cheap," the city said. "Your eyes are the eyes of the others. Only to you I mean a little more because you know me, have lived in me, and you understand my heart. For you, however, I still have nothing, because you give nothing to me. The joke's on you. Tear your heart out, sucker."

When Janik reached the outside of the car, he found himself in the company of the conductor, who, having a few seconds ago announced the stop, was ready to swing open the door between cars and place down his portable half-step the minute the train stopped.

"Looks like you're the only one gettin' off," said the conductor, glancing back over Janik's shoulder.

"Yeah."

"Live here?"

"Nope."

"I used to," volunteered the conductor. "Down on Third Avenue, South Side. Was born and grew up there. Worked in the paper mills when I was a kid. Yes, sir. Hard work, I mean."

"Yeah?"

"Yep. Me and the missus moved to the city when all the kids got married and moved away."

"Yeah?"

"Yep. Kinda miss it, though, this town," said the conductor.

"Yeah?"

"Yep," said the conductor. "Hard to explain. Guess you never get away from the place you first grew up . . . no matter where you go."

The complete stop of the train automatically disengaged their conversation.

As Janik stepped off the train at the *Herald News* sign and started up the walk to go through the station down to the street, some of the old strength seemed to find its way inside him and he felt that for the first time in a long time he could see colors again instead of everything being just black or white or a dirty muddled gray. He hadn't written anything in two years.

It was crazy.

He knew that.

And anybody that didn't have an artist's sensitivity wouldn't understand it.

On the other hand, he had to admit that the feeling wasn't necessarily indicative of the end result.

He thought back to the many times he had gotten this over-the-brim-I-can-conquer-anything feeling and attempted to write and strained and sweated and struggled with himself only to wind up with a complete blank. A lot of words on a lot of paper, but none of it was the true him.

But disregarding these nil periods and false starts he felt that if he just had a pencil and paper in his hands right now he could write indefinitely. And all meat, too. Not the kind of unhealthy fat you came up with when you weren't "on" and had to push yourself.

Janik remembered he had felt imbued with this superman confidence most of the time during the year he had lived here while he was working at the Ordnance Ammunition Command and roughing out *High above the Earth.* He had written more than half of it right here in Joliet.

Writing had seemed like the easiest and most natural thing in the world after he had first seen Joan.

Every compulsive word of every compulsive sentence of every compulsive page was written to her and of her, and the chances were that she probably never even knew it.

There was a fabulous story in it somewhere.

He was more than halfway to the station when he became consciously aware of the bells.

He halted abruptly and listened.

It was close to four years since he had been here last, and he had almost forgotten about the bells.

All the encyclopedias and research books about Joliet provided you with barrels of information and cut-and-dried facts about population, newspapers, waterways, railroads, industries, the location of Stateville, what streets and how many blocks comprised the Loop, what weeknight the stores were open late on, etc., etc., etc., but nowhere in any book did you find one single solitary word about the bells and they were more the heart and identifying characteristic of the city than any other single element in it.

Janik listened more intently and took a bearing.

From where he was standing it sounded like they were coming from somewhere up on the West Side.

St. John's probably.

Funny . . .

He remembered what a shiver, a shiver that greatness always inspired in him, he had felt run through him when he had first read Janney's *Miracle of the Bells.*

The chance meeting in a hick town in Iowa on Christmas Eve between the press agent, the advance man for the road company, and the chorus girl he had met only once before.

Standing there, talking to her awhile in the street, then taking her to the local deserted chowmienery for dinner and really getting to know her and steering her to the top.

And she constantly remembering him in her thoughts because he had taken notice of her and spoken up on her behalf when she was only a no-'count tangle-footed hoofer, sweating for rent money, trying to make the line in a New York girlie show.

"Give the kid a break," Spats Dunnigan had said on a hunch, "Give the kid a break."

She never forgot it. Not even after she became a big star for Marcus Harris.

And then the press agent bringing the girl's emaciated, self-destroyed body back to the Pennsylvania mining town where she was born and grew up, back to Coaltown, back among the people she knew and loved, to bury her in the shadow of the breaker and the slag heap, the symbols of slavery and oppression she hated.

And through it all giving himself a million kinds of hell, punishing himself with every mental bludgeon because he had never told her how he felt about her when she was alive and certainly would never have that chance again now that she was dead. Janik had read the book three times and seen the picture four.

To him Alida Valli was the greatest actress in the world. You could just tell by looking at her that the woman had depth.

Back there at the early age in Jersey when he had first read it he thought that it would have been the most wonderful thing in the world to be stuck in a small Midwestern town like that during the Holy Season, when everything was peaceful and quiet, and just be able to wander around aimlessly, free-mindedly, without knowing anybody and without anybody knowing you and let the anonymity of the night dictate the terms for the evening.

And now, ironically enough, here he was after all.

Not in Iowa on Christmas Eve wondering what to do with himself between now and the time that the milk train went out early the next morning, not in Coaltown to bury the short-changed Olga Treskovna.

It was Joliet he was looking down on now, and *Miracle of the Bells*, great as it was, was only an insignificant book on a library shelf listed under "J."

He was alone and cold and lonely. Those things were the same. But the situation was nowhere as lofty and his thoughts were nowhere as "free-minded" as he imagined they would be.

Janik readjusted his scarf higher around his neck, pulled his topcoat up even with his ears, and started walking again toward the station with his head bent down against the butt of the wind, wondering if there really was a woman anywhere on the face of this earth that was as kind and unselfish and dedicated as Olga Treskovna.

The bells, flaring out over the city from somewhere up on the West Side, St. John's probably, had brought it all back so clearly.

When Janik got down to the street he immediately crossed over to the west side of Scott and anxiously quick-paced the half-block to the side entrance of the Woodruff. He had to get in somewhere before his ears fell off.

He had realized it was cold. It was cold in Chicago, but nothing like this.

Joliet, he knew from past experience, was always ten degrees one way or the other compared to Chicago.

If it was eighty-five in July up there, it'd be ninety-five down here. If it was twenty in Chicago in January, it'd be ten in Joliet. You could count on it.

When he got inside he turned to his left before he hit the lobby and navigated the three steps down into the Green Room. It was practically deserted.

There was only a young bartender leisurely wiping imaginary specks of dirt off of glasses he had polished earlier in the afternoon, two gun-jumping drunks choking in a common laughter over a dirty joke, and three inactive waitresses huddled around a corner table eating like savages.

Janik steered to his left away from the rummies and settled at the far end of the bar, positioning himself so that he could have a clean shot at the entranceway, exploiting the possibility that he might spot somebody he knew going by and he'd be able to ask about Joan.

How she was.

What she looked like.

The things she said.

Anything.

He took off his scarf and topcoat and draped them around a wire hanger on the clothes rack behind him.

When he turned around he found himself face to face with the young bartender, a sleek Italiano who had the name "Tony" neatly embroidered directly above the right pocket of his white-on-white Hathaway.

"Bardolino, Tony."

"What?"

"Bardolino."

"Never heard of it."

"Make it Chianti then. Bring the bottle. And a beer glass."

"A beer glass?" Tony hesitated.

"Yeah."

"Oh. We drink it the same way home with supper lotta times. First time anybody ever asked for it here, though."

"Yeah?"

"Yeah. In this joint most of our wine customers are broads who sit here and sip their drinks outta them tiny mushroom glasses with their pinkies up in the air."

"Real talent, huh?"

"Yeah," laughed Tony. "Don't ask me what the hell they get out of it either. They make me nervous."

Tony went and got the wine from out of the cooler beneath the bar, picked up a beer glass out of a row he had set up on a fresh towel, laid it in front of Janik, and carefully filled it to the brim.

"How much do you want?" said Janik, reaching for the roll in his pocket and peeling off a tentative five.

"Well, I don't know," said Tony, scratching his head uncertainly. "Nobody ever asked me for a beer glass fulla wine before. Not in here. Tell you what," he said after a moment's pause. "Tell you what," he said looking over his shoulder. "I'll tell you what. I'll charge you half a buck a glass. What the hell." He gestured recklessly. "It's New Year's Eve. Drink up!"

Janik emptied his glass to about half an inch from the bottom without taking a breath and shivered all over as the wine chilled him with its bitterness before it started to warm him with its sweetness.

The bartender filled his glass to the top again, Janik took another good deep slug, and only smiled indulgently when

Tony, watching him curiously, reminded him that the stuff, when drunk that fast, was bad.

Bad? thought Janik. *It's all bad.*

The whole goddamn mess that passes off as existence, it's bad.

The hypocrisy . . . the perfidy . . . the rejection . . . the shallow single-mindedness of the powerful petty bourgeois . . . the emptiness of success all combining to wear us down to suicide edge.

Happy New Year, he thought.

Happy, happy, happy New Year, everybody. May you live to be a hundred, and God bless you one and all.

Janik only smiled indulgently and took another slug.

He just sat there by himself after that, and kept drinking. By the time he was in the middle of his third glass, which he decided to sip, the place was starting to fill.

As a matter of fact, it was beginning to get absolutely crowded. There were no more available stools at the bar, and people just coming in were forced to stand wherever there was an opening or sit at the tables in the rear normally reserved for dining.

Janik had not really noticed when all these people had come in. In between heavy slugs of wine and heavy sighs of regret over a hopeless love he had not noticed anything at all.

It was really like a magic trick, this influx. One minute there was nobody and then the very next second practically half of Joliet.

They had seemingly snuck up and, as if by some predetermined signal during a well-planned attack, advanced on the Green Room in a concentrated drive.

And now, after successfully capturing their objective, they were looting and pillaging, drinking and brawling, singing and boasting in wild exuberation over their triumph.

Janik just sat back with his wine in his hand and watched them rock on their heels.

What a painting it would make, he thought. *Joliet at Night.*

It would never make the cover of *Look,* not even the back page. Just a bunch of isolated must that nobody would ever think worthwhile to photograph or write about in a million years.

What did America care what was going on in Joliet?

What did America care what was going on in America?

You did your job, spent your money, drank your liquor, and made your women without thinking what the hell it all meant in terms of utopias, discontent, pyramids, artifacts, the magic carpet, and the Zodiac.

Anybody played it any other way was an intellectual, an outcast, a dullard, and a creep.

There was the proof of himself stretching out before him, reflecting off each motion and uttered word as sharply and acutely as the multitude of colors in a rotating diamond.

Janik had not kept track of the amount of time he had spent at the Woodruff. It didn't seem like more than an hour and a half, two hours maybe.

He looked around and couldn't spot a clock.

The last train back to Chicago was 10:30, on the Alton, but he had not yet decided whether he would be sane about the whole thing and make it or be his usual unflinching, unreasonable self and make a night of it.

He knew only too well that if he did get the early train back to Chicago he would feel empty and cheated and more lost than he felt coming down.

And when he did get into La Salle Street Station at 11:30 or so it would be too late to start off anywhere and he would wind up seeing in the New Year at one of the assorted second-rate dives on Van Buren.

On the other hand, the next train out after the 10:30 was the 6:01 in the morning.

He could soothe his tortured soul in Joliet here at the Woodruff and the Louis Joliet until he became blind from the drink and eventually wound up sleeping on the hardwood at Union Station until the train went out in the morning. He had done it before a couple of times ten years ago. Even slept right through the 6:01 and gotten the 7:02.

Right now, after another big slug of wine, he just didn't know. . . .

Janik took another futile look around the room for a clock. He knew there was one in a lobby in front of the desk, but he considered it too much of an effort for the decision he had to make.

Instead of asking anyone, he turned around, put on his coat, and walked none too steadily out the door and started to slant across Scott back to the station.

In the middle of the street he suddenly changed his mind, figuring the hell with it, who knew when he'd be down here again, and turned and went back north up Scott and across Jefferson two blocks farther to the Louis Joliet.

When he got inside the Louis the situation wasn't much different from that at the Woodruff.

It was a little more subdued; a smaller room, a different crowd, still open and disjointed, but considerably less ribald.

Janik moved his way around, following the curve of the bar, and just managed to grab one of the two seats that were evacuated by a couple who were making the rounds and had had their fill of the place.

He was beginning to feel just a bit sick and out of it from all the wine he had drunk so fast at the Woodruff and at this point didn't especially care for anymore.

Consequently when the bartender asked him what he wanted he told him that he was Walter W. Janik, the one and only and newest and brightest star on the American literary horizon come back home to Joliet to absorb and recapture a little full-headedness and life-meaning to neutralize and cancel out the cheapness and big-time phoniness of the greatest city in the world, so would he mind very much if he just sat there very quietly and absorbed and recaptured?

"Another drunk nut," said the bartender, shaking his head sadly. He moved away to serve another customer at the other end of the bar.

When the bartender had given the other customer his drink and was on his way to ring it up on the register Janik reached out and grabbed him by the arm.

"How about a Seven N Seven?" he said.

"You're drunk, buddy," said the bartender. "Why don't you go and sleep it off somewhere?"

"C'mon," said Janik seriously, "gimme a drink, I ain't drunk. Can't you tell when a guy's actin'?"

The bartender pulled his hand away from Janik's loose grip, took out for the drink, and gave the other customer his change.

"How about that drink?" persisted Janik.

"You're green around the gills, kid," said the bartender. "Why don't you just go home?"

"C'mon, friend. I told ya I was only kiddin' with the bit. All I had to drink tonight was a couple glasses of wine. I swear."

"You don't look too hot."

"C'mon. Givus a drink, huh? Christ, it's New Year's Eve."

The bartender just stared at Janik shrewdly without saying a word.

"Okay, kid," he said finally. "One drink and if you start to feel light, don't pass out here. One drink," he said, pointing a finger, "just one drink."

"Don't worry, pal. I know this town pretty good. If I feel

light there are plenty a side streets I can crawl down and die in complete obscurity. Now how about that drink?"

"What was it again?"

"Seven N Seven."

The bartender gave him his drink and Janik gulped it down while looking directly in the length of the bar mirror in front of him to see if he might recognize anybody sitting at any of the tables in the rear.

"One more," he said, tapping his glass lightly on the bar. "Gimme a refill."

"Take it easy, kid," admonished the bartender. "You drink that stuff like water."

"Well, I'm parched," said Janik. "I didn't realize it. That wine is wors'n drinkin' sand."

He was halfway through his second drink when he thought he spotted a girl he had known at OAC sitting at one of the group tables in the rear.

He thought it was a girl named Rita who had worked in Payroll a couple of doors down the corridor from his own office on the first floor. He thought so, but he wasn't sure.

The faces and figures of a person's youth were only a loan that time repaid into maturity.

The girl looked very familiar at a certain angle, but when she turned her head and Janik caught her face full on she looked like a total stranger. A little heavier certainly and without the carefree mannerisms of the girl he had known.

Still, he thought he had caught her staring at him a couple of times in the mirror with that suspended "where have I seen you before?" look.

He forgot about it and ordered another drink.

While Janik was drinking he made it a point not to say anything to anybody because he was afraid that he'd provoke or get provoked into an argument and get kicked out.

And if he was forced to leave, with the exception of a

couple of bars way up on Ottowa, there was nowhere else he could go.

Actually, keeping quiet wasn't too hard, because he was rapidly reaching the point where it was difficult to say one word. He had drunk so much over at the Woodruff and here that he no longer felt bloated or satiated or anything.

Just numb.

He had caught himself drifting off a couple of times, losing his awareness, but had jerked himself upright each time and forced himself to stay awake.

This last time, after his fifth or sixth drink, he had lowered his head flat on the bar without realizing it, regained his senses, twisted himself upward, and clamorously asked for another drink.

The bartender took his glass without saying a word, wiped the bar clean in front of him, and moved out from behind it.

He came up in back of Janik, grabbed him under the arms, lifted him off the stool, and guided him out of the Joliet Room into the lobby, onto one of the sofas in front of the fireplace.

Janik, drunk and resistless, lay there as ridiculous and useless as an abused and out-of-date rag doll.

"Do you know anybody in there that can take you home?" asked the bartender.

"Huh?"

"I said is there anybody around here you know—"

"Don't holler. I heard you the first time. I ain't deaf."

"Well?"

"Well what?"

"Is there?"

"Is there what?"

"Anybody who can give you a lift home."

"The Damms."

"Who?"

"The Damms."

"Who're they?"

"Mr. Damm and Mrs. Damm and the Damm kids two or three . . . an' U. B. Damn an' I. B. Damm an' the whole Damm fam—"

"Okay, okay," said the bartender. "Where do you live? I'll get you a cab."

"Huh?"

"I said where do you live? I'll get—"

"Don't holler. Who the hell you think you're talkin' to?"

"Look, kid. I don't care one way or the other. You want a cab or not? You understand what I'm sayin'?"

"Right."

"Then where do you live?"

"Philly."

"Where?"

"East Philadelphia."

"Okay," said the bartender. "Stay here and sleep it off. I don't think anybody'll say anything."

Janik turned over on his stomach, forced off his shoes toe to heel, and buried his head in the comforting darkness of his elbow.

Actually, he didn't know how long he lay there before the racket caved in on his ears. It could have been only a few seconds, and then again he might have dozed off and come to again.

But when it happened it actually seemed like the whole of Joliet had suddenly triggered itself and erupted.

Bells started to ring, whistles started to blow, noisemakers started to rasp, horns started to toot, music started to play, and drunks started to holler.

Bromfield would have called it a cacophony.

A helluva thing, thought Janik.

A helluva, helluva, helluva thing when the alcohol ate

through the will and made us its inert prisoner. There would have been so much to see. So much to retain. If only he hadn't done all that early drinking to drown out the emptiness.

Maybe he could still make it if he forced himself.

Try, Janik. Try. Get up and move. Give it that extra burst like going from first to third on a single. Show them your speed.

Inside his brain he tried and commanded and strained, but no matter what mental contortions he went through in the attempt to extricate himself, he couldn't make a move.

He was like a snowbound car encased in a deep snowdrift, motor gunning to full rpm, wheels spinning like crazy, but going nowhere.

What a way to wind up, he thought. *What a goddamn silly way to wind up.*

What a sight.

What a sickening sight you must be, Janik.

If they could only see you now. The ones who look up to you and respect you and hang onto your every word. The ones who always try to use their best grammar whenever you're around and the ones you try to humanize yourself to by using your worse.

The typists and the waitresses, the dockhands and the truck drivers on the South and West sides of Chicago who have you into their homes to sit at their tables and eat their food and proudly tell their friends and relatives the next morning what a warm and regular guy you are.

The ones about whom you talk passionately of uplifting and secretly despise as the powerful petty bourgeoisie.

And the very same ones who have more decency, self-respect, and common good in the tips of their little fingers than you got in your whole body.

Walter W. Janik.

The people's champion.

The fabulous novelist.

What a laugh!

If they only knew what a scared and bewildered punk you really were inside.

The constant indecision, depression, and flirtation with suicide.

The loneliness and the sorrow, the bitterness and the hate. The sleepless nights and the wait for night.

If any one of them only knew.

PART II

THE WEST SIDE

As the night ripened into maturity, the lights in the windows of Joliet's houses blinked off and on like an armada of lightning bugs. Behind them, people ran the gamut of human emotion in their preparation for the night's action.

They talked freely about the old year and wondered how it could have gone by so quickly, where it had fled. They thought about it and silently degraded themselves for their inertia and lack of accomplishment.

Above everything, they made up their minds that this coming year would be different. This time they had a plan and they would stick to it. The big money was just around the corner. This scheme simply couldn't fail.

But that was the future. That was tomorrow and the day after. Right now there was this very night to mull over and think about. Where to go and what to do. What to wear and what time to get there. Everybody had definite ideas and no two people were the same.

Some had decided that they would spend a quiet evening at home and avoid all the noisy crowds, the pushing and pulling, the restless carousing, and the inane foolishness of any drunken gathering.

Nothing special. Just a few friends in from the office for a few drinks, some social generalizing, and then early to bed.

Still others, mostly the unbridled unmarried element, planned to go out and drink the town dry.

Anybody that stayed in on a night like this, didn't avail himself of the opportunities that such a night afforded, was either a jerk or a square. How else could you figure it?

It was New Year's Eve, U.S.A., and while this wasn't, say, Times Square, State and Randolph, Collins Avenue, or the Strip, a person could still have one hell of a time without even trying. People, after all, were people, no matter where you went.

Staying in was senseless. Definitely. Above and beyond. Close to criminal.

And then, as always, in any element, gathering, group, or society there were those who simply couldn't make up their minds.

They would very much like to go out if only they could get the grandmother to come over and sit with the baby. The old lady hadn't been feeling too well herself and had begged off when she was asked last week. Your life wasn't your own when you had to depend on somebody else.

Maybe the old lady was feeling good enough to come over for just a little while to see that the kid was tucked in when he got tired. A baby, especially a tiny infant, was such a terrific responsibility.

Then again, they wondered if it would be right and worth all the trouble to hustle off their own flesh and blood on an unwanting old lady just for a few hours' pleasure. She would probably come and watch if they asked her hard enough. She always did. Sick or not.

But the truth was they were not really sure that they had wanted a child in the first place. It was a nice thing to have, but your youth didn't last forever and New Year's came only once a year.

They sat down around the kitchen table and discussed it.

All over the city elements of catalyst were in various stages of development, adding a touch of this or a drop of that to the overall potion, hoping that it would bring about the desired effect to the carefully prearranged or hit-and-miss target for tonight.

In the bedroom of a large white frame house on the high ground of the West Side of Joliet sat a remarkably pretty young woman staring at her own image in the center of a mirror.

She was, she had been told by more than a few men on more than a few occasions, the most beautiful woman they had ever seen . . . a fact that did not move or impress her to any great extent, because she had known just that exact same thing ever since she had first become conscious of herself in her early teens.

Telling Joan Henry that she was beautiful was like giving a million dollars to the richest man in the world. It was a lot of money, but so what?

If this Croesus was what he was and had what he obviously had, the chances are that he didn't get it hustling insurance door to door or selling chestnuts in Times Square to get started. Chances are he was born with most of it and had built it up from there.

It was the same thing with Joan Henry. Joan Henry had always had looks.

When she was a child it was always "you cute little this" and "you adorable little that." Then when she grew up and started going with men it was invariably "your beauty exceeds this" and "whenever I'm with you you make me feel that."

Not that she truthfully minded being told that she was pretty. What woman did? Even if she was plain and it was a lie. It was just that she had never met anybody that had ever made her feel on the inside the way she knew she looked from without.

Well, not quite anybody.

There had been one. How long ago was it now? Three . . . four years? It seemed like a million.

How many times during that period had she gone over it in her mind, from beginning to end, from end to beginning, examining it every which way, trying to chisel out some wedge of understanding, only to see the whole thing remain unanswerably intact in its frustrating continuity.

With Joan Henry it had been an immediate thing. One look and she had gone completely overboard. She had read about things like this, but she did not believe that it could ever happen to her.

In the first place, it wasn't her conception of love. Everything that had ever been impressed upon her by training and upbringing told her that it was wrong. A woman didn't go around losing her head over a total stranger that walked in and out of the blue without knowing anything about him.

But there it was there was no sense fighting it. From out of nowhere . . . one look . . . and suddenly everything made sense.

Back there in the beginning she used to look for him and wait for him to approach her, but he never did. After a while she even stopped looking, because whenever their eyes met and held whatever it was used to rush to her head and dent her composure and she had to break it off.

As the days went by and one month blended into another he made no attempt to know her or to break the ice.

There was a department dance at the Joliet Arsenal—a legitimate opening—he didn't even show up. If he passed her in the hall he would look right through her as if she didn't even exist. On the average she only saw him once every two or three weeks. Never more.

Curiously enough, because of this lack, instead of the desire and the need diminishing, it increased. Joan Henry had never known anything like this before, and she hated him because she thought he was a snob. He had this vicelike grip on her without even trying, and it maddened her because that was what she wanted, but not like this.

She was still mad the night he called her, and she hung up in his face when he said he wanted to see her.

She cut him short on purpose, because in the first place she wasn't sure if it was him, and if it was then she wanted to hurt him and cut him up just like he was doing to her every time she passed him in the hall.

Joan looked for him after that. Consistently. Even went out of her way on phony details just so she could walk past his office in the hope of seeing him, but he wasn't around. She didn't know what happened, but she didn't have to wonder long.

When it broke it seemed like everybody at OAC knew about it at the same time.

No two people received and retold the story in the same manner, but the general impression that filtered down was that he was at the Veterans Hospital down in Dwight and that there was something wrong with his throat.

Some said it was tonsils. Still others said it was laryngitis. An easily susceptible person said it was a bad cold. An old lady softly whispered cancer.

Barbara Hall over in Personnel was the one who told Joan Henry about it.

It was all there in the records, Barbara said. Ten point-disability . . . singer . . . vocal cord polypectomy . . . San Antonio, May 1953 . . . Air Force . . . aviation cadet. . . . It was all there in black and white. Easily the most engrossing Form 57 in the entire file.

As the rest of it trailed off into monotony Joan Henry felt she wanted to crawl inside herself and pull the zipper shut.

During the next few days she thought about it constantly, and little by little it all began to make sense. All the pieces began to fit. The constant snubs. The total withdrawal. The triple steel front. The pain in the eyes. All of it because of a real hard unimaginary reason.

Joan Henry sat through each day torturing herself with

it and decided that if he was dying in the hospital she didn't care, because she was dying out here.

Altogether Janik was in the hospital two weeks and back at OAC one before she got the chance to see him.

He was coming down the corridor and she was going up, and as she gauged it, she saw that he would have to pass her before he reached the side corridor where he would turn off to his own office. Joan came up to him, and she stopped completely, not half-stopped or slowed down, but stopped completely and reached out for his arm and said, "Hello," and Walter Janik just brushed right by her, looking straight ahead, as if she didn't even exist.

On Tuesday of the third week Barbara Hall came rushing down from Personnel to tell her that he had just had some kind of argument with Patterson, the section head, and had just walked out and said that he was going back home, back east, for good.

Barbara hadn't been there personally, she said, but the way she got it they had just been sitting there in the office, talking normally, when suddenly both of them had flared.

Patterson had backed down quickly and had right away tried to smooth things over, pleaded with Janik, promised him an upgrading to a GS-5 as soon as he could get the papers through, but he wouldn't listen. Janik wouldn't listen.

He just threw it over in one grand gesture, Barbara said. No resignation, no formality, no nothing. Just threw down his identification tag and walked out.

Inside herself Joan Henry cheered. So Janik had just thrown it over and walked out, had he? Just like that? Fabulous!

How many times had she wanted to do just that very same thing herself? Just get up and walk out and show them that your whole life wasn't hinged upon your total submission to the puerile whims of some overstuffed parvenu.

That was the way to quit. Just tell some pompous jerk to take his job and shove it whether you could afford to or not.

But now he was gone. That was the end result, and Joan Henry knew that it would be rough from here on in.

You only fell in love once in your life, truly and completely. All the rest were only reasonable facsimiles that you conditioned yourself into believing out of necessity.

Nothing endures and Joan Henry wondered how long it would be before the thought of him faded and she didn't see his face every time she closed her eyes.

There would be others. Probably many. She was only twenty-one. But as the weeks went by and he wasn't around she stopped fighting him and he became more deeply embedded in her memory than ever.

Almost four years, she thought, bringing herself back into focus once again in the mirror. She hadn't seen him now for four years, and it seemed just like yesterday.

She had read a lot about him in the papers, of course.

The worldwide acclaim, personal appearances, his novel in the front row of every bookstore window, the article in *Life*, and so on.

She had even seen him on "Person to Person" a few months ago, and he looked even younger on television than he did in the picture that the wire services carried when he won the Pulitzer Prize.

A boy.

Deadly serious, though. She could never remember having seen him smile.

Joan Henry's mind drifted back to him time and time again with frightening regularity of late, and she couldn't help wondering if she had sold herself out.

Outwardly Joan Henry realized that she was the envy of everybody she came in contact with.

She lived in the finest white house in the best part of town, wore only the most expensive clothes bought a Korshak's and Beth Fritz's on Michigan Boulevard and worked because she was bored. On top of that she had a kind and devoted husband well established in business and in the community.

Whenever they went out for dinner or to a show, people always turned their heads in their direction in open admiration and whispered what a handsome and well-suited couple they made.

Outwardly Joan Henry had everything. Outwardly.

Inwardly Joan Henry was a very self-disillusioned young woman who had once promised herself that she would only marry for love and had settled for that much detested and despised, very necessary reasonable facsimile.

Inwardly she wondered what kind of a marriage she had made herself a partner to. Sleeping in one man's bed and thinking of another.

If you were a single girl and sold your services to the highest bidder, society damned you and branded you a slut. You were ostracized and shunned by the respectable core of law-abiding citizens wherever you went. The decision had been made. From this there was no appeal.

If you were a single girl and did the very same thing but took the trouble to dignify it with a marriage, the very same people who condemned you would be moved to tears. They would say you captured a prize and shake their heads and cluck their teeth with respect to how smart and clever you were.

And with that ring on your finger you could hold up your head in any company. Any company, that is, but your own. You couldn't kid yourself.

Basically you weren't any better than a fancy tramp.

Wherever you went there was something to remind you what a complete sham it was. A sham and a fool's paradise that had begun to wear off even before you stood together on Saturday afternoon in front of the priest.

Everything pales with familiarity, but this marriage had started to lose its color even before the honeymoon. The only reason she had gone through with it was because the time was ripe and there was nothing else. Nothing real.

It hadn't changed anything, though. As a matter of fact it even made things worse. She was even more dead inside now than she had ever been before. But there was no way out. No alternative. No revocability.

If she broke it off now she would have even less than she had before. But even more than that, she would have to bear the stigma of a divorced woman. And in a town like this . . .

Inwardly Joan Henry wondered if she had enough courage to try it. How far gone and how deep in did a person have to be before he went over the edge?

What a splash it would make, she thought: What a paradox it would be. Her picture on the front page of all the newspapers, sprawled out on the floor in maybe a bathrobe or a slip with the wrists slashed, the hair mussed, a trail of blood all over the room, everything disarrayed but the face, that serious face, that perfect face, that paragon of a face that many men had told her was the most beautiful face in the world.

Joan Henry could just see them gasping in disbelief.

"Wife of prominent West Side executive a suicide!" the *Spectator* would scream.

"West Side beauty in mystery death," the *Herald News* would vie.

Back and forth it would go. Day after day. Week after week. Month after month. All the statements and misstatements, the speculation, the conjecture, the gossip. What a shot in the arm it would be. They'd be talking about it for years. And nobody would ever figure it either.

Nobody.

How could they? Anybody who had eyes could see that this was a girl who had everything.

She lived in the finest white house in the best part of town, wore only the most expensive clothes, bought at Korshak's and Beth Fritz's on Michigan Boulevard, and had a kind and devoted husband well established in business and in the community.

Outwardly she had everything.

Outwardly.

Inwardly Joan Henry was a very self-disillusioned young woman who had once promised herself that she would only marry for love and had settled for that much detested and despised very necessary reasonable facsimile. So what people didn't know, what nobody knew, what probably nobody would ever know, was that inwardly Joan Henry had nothing. Absolutely nothing.

"Hi, Joanie."

Joan wheeled around and saw her husband walking into the room working off his gloves.

"You scared me, Spence. When did you come in?"

"Just now. Didn't you hear me? I made enough noise coming up the stairs to wake up the dead."

"Oh? What time is it?"

"Almost a quarter to ten. Come on. Hurry up. How come you're not dressed?"

"Dressed for what?"

"Dressed for what? What're you kidding? What's the joke?"

"No, I'm not kidding and it's no joke."

Spencer Henry stared at his wife for a moment with a half-smile on his face and then laughed.

"Okay, honey, c'mon," he said. "Fun's fun. You wearing the white dress you bought in Chicago?"

"I'm not in a very white mood tonight."

"Well then, what are you wearing?"

"Nothing."

"What kind of an answer is that?"

"Just what the hell it sounds like."

"You mean you're not going?"

"The force of your precocity has hit the gong. You get a cigar, buster."

"I could do without the glib dialogue."

"Yeah? Well, I may remove the source quicker than you think."

"Look Joanie, this is crazy. What are we fighting about? Put on the white dress and let's get out of here. You haven't been out of the house since before Thanksgiving. Come on."

"Nobody's fighting, Spence. I'm just telling you. I'm not going out tonight. So let's drop it."

"Be reasonable, Joanie. We have to go. Everybody's expecting us. How will it look?"

"I don't know," said Joan blankly. "Probably like we don't give a damn."

"Well, what are you gonna do?"

"I'm going to sit right here, turn on the phonograph, listen to as many records as I can, and get drunk by myself. How's that?"

"Joanie, be serious. The reservations are made; the plans are set; everybody'll be looking for us. What's come over you? What'll everybody think?"

"They'll think exactly what you lead them to think when you get there."

"When I get there," said Spence dumbfoundedly. "You mean without you?"

"That's right, Spence" Joan said. "Without me."

"What makes you think I'd go without you? What makes you think I'd even consider it?"

"Well, you just got done saying the reservations are made, the plans are set. It sounds like the curtain going up on act one. How will it look?"

Spencer Henry came around and sat down on the edge of the stool beside his wife. He sat there uncertainly for a moment and then placed his arm lightly around her shoulder.

"What's wrong, Joanie? Why the sudden change? Why don't you want to go?"

Joan sighed heavily, jerked away from him, and walked across the room to the window overlooking the street.

"I just don't, that's all. And I don't want to talk about it anymore either. If you want to go, that's fine. And get off the stool and let me sit down, unless you want to powder your nose."

"What's wrong, Joanie? Something's eating you. You're hurting about something. I can tell. I can see it. Have I done something? Is it me?"

She turned back to him and suddenly felt very sorry for him because he looked so hurt and bewildered and lost. It suddenly occurred to her what a hard and impossible thing it must be for him to understand something she couldn't understand herself.

"Look Spence," she said, "you just go out and have your good time. Forget everything else. It'll do you good."

Spencer Henry got up from his sitting position and started to walk up to his wife.

"Joanie . . . "

"Look," she erupted, veering away, "what are we, strangers? Two fumbling kids on our wedding night? We've been married four years now, and you know me well enough to know when I mean what I say."

"I know, Joanie; I know. It's just that it'll look funny if we aren't there. I mean the preparations and everything. I took it for granted."

"Nobody's asking you to sit home," stated Joan. "You can go out and do whatever you please."

"Joanie look," said Spencer Henry, brightly, "don't go on my account. Think of all your friends. What'll they think?"

"My friends," said Joan Henry, "can go to hell as far as I'm concerned. And I'm sick and tired of governing my actions by other people's standards just to prove that I'm a suitable wife for you."

"The way you talk," said Spencer Henry, shaking his head sadly.

"You ought to be grateful they can't hear you talk this way."

"Spare me the hearts and flowers," Joan said. "They're your friends, not mine. Almost every one. Snide and snippy and small. And tonight won't be any different than any other night."

"What do you mean?"

"What do I mean? What do you think I mean? They'll all sit there in judgment and watch each other like a bunch of vultures to see if anybody drinks too much or says the wrong thing just so they can have something to pick apart tomorrow morning.

"Them and their high-blown standards. They all think this world begins and ends with this crummy town . . . and for them it does . . and they'll rot in it, too."

"And you along with them, Joanie?"

"And me along with them," said Joan unhesitatingly. "I'm just as bad. I can't get away from it either. But at least I know it."

"Then you won't go?"

Joan started to tell him for what seemed like the thirty-eighth time when some abstract force unexpectedly pushed her outside herself and made her an objective third party taking in both sides of the story, and she laughed almost convulsively at the ridiculous absurdity of it all.

"Look, Spence," she said, catching her breath. "Look," she said. "This is beginning to drag. Talking to you is the hardest work I know. If you don't hurry up and get dressed and get out there you'll miss your chance to nuzzle somebody else's wife."

Spencer Henry lowered his head and started walking out of the room. The whole thing was just too much.

When he reached the door he stopped and turned around.

"I never knew," he said. "I honestly never realized you felt this way about any of it. Not until now."

"Oh, I felt it," Joan said. "I felt it more than once. Only I never felt remote enough or depressed enough to say it."

"I never knew," said Spencer Henry.

"Well, now you know," said his wife.

"Is there anything you want? Anything I can get you before I go?"

"Like what?"

"I don't know," said Spencer Henry blankly. "Anything."

"I've got everything I need, thanks. Everything but what I want."

"What?"

"Skip it," snapped Joan.

Accepting the fact that further discussion would get him nowhere, Spencer Henry wheeled around and walked dejectedly into the next room. He took his tuxedo out of the closet and laid it out on the bed and started to peel off the dark business suit he had worked in and worn throughout the day.

He did not like what he had just heard. He did not like it one bit. But he loved his wife very much. Loved her almost to the point of worship and, being aware of her strong independence, was reluctant to assert himself too demandingly.

He governed himself with the knowledge that his wife, as an only child, was used to having her own way and that any gap that developed between them over some small and relatively unimportant thing might very conceivably widen itself into a yawning abyss that would be impossible to bridge later on.

And there were guys stacked up on the street corners of the world waiting to snap up women like Joan Henry.

Before she married him she could have had her pick. She still could, as far as that went . . . and he knew it. His wife was, without a doubt, the most beautiful woman he had ever seen.

Beautiful and temperamental.

This wasn't the first time he had seen her in this kind of a mood. The first time was shortly after they were married. She would go off on a tangent for no reason and be impossible to live with for a while, and then she would come back down to earth and everything would be all right until it happened again.

Not understanding it, Henry chose to ignore it and would generally make himself scarce until whatever was eating away at her had run its course.

But here in the past six months her behavior had become consistently erratic, and the most basic relationship between a man and his wife had ceased to exist.

Now as they moved about the house together, woke up to each other's faces in the morning, sat down to dinner at night, they were like two people with familiar faces who, not having seen each other for a number of years, pass on the street, stop and think, then look back and try to remember where they were friends.

Spencer Henry did not like it, but he was afraid that if he opened his mouth and pushed her too far she would pack up and leave. And if she left she'd mean it, too. She was that kind of a girl.

Even tonight, when he saw that she was "off," he didn't want to say anything. But one thing had led to another, and he had let it get away from him.

Maybe, in a sense, it was a good thing to talk about it and let her get it out of her system. Now he knew at least a part of what was eating her.

When he finished dressing, he took one final look in the mirror to run a comb through his hair and straighten his tie. In the same move that he made the final adjustment he glanced at his watch and saw that he was more than a half hour late. The night would be half-over if he didn't make a little time.

As he walked out of his room and by the open door of Joan's, he saw her lying there resting her eyes. He stood there a minute watching the regularity of her breathing and then went quickly down the stairs and out of the house.

Back upstairs when Joan heard the front door slam she got up out of bed, went to the window, and peeked down into the street from behind the edge of the blind.

She saw her husband get into the Buick, drive off, and disappear around the curve in the road just the other side of St. John's Church.

Joan came away from the window, turned off the light, and sprawled herself out on the bed. She stopped on the way to light a cigarette and lift an ashtray, which she took the trouble to center on her stomach once she had herself settled.

Then she shifted her cigarette to her left hand and reached over to the night table and turned on the radio.

It was an RCA portable, the kind where the sound came on immediately, and it exploded throughout the room before she had a chance to turn it down.

Joan didn't listen to the radio too much anymore.

The radio was her youth that had somehow gotten lost in

the maddening drive of higher horsepower, television, drive-in theaters, lighter beer, and cooler smokes.

It was a luxury just to lie there with her eyes closed and let the music carry her off. A luxury that excluded thought and decision.

For no special reason, when she turned it on it was right on the local station, WJOL. When she heard it was Gleason she left it right there.

They were playing "I'll Never be the Same" from his *Lonesome Echoes* album. The one with the mandolins.

Fabulous, the effect he got with those mandolins.

They were all sundown.

Every one of them.

A million weary workers showing their drag and their hurt at the end of the day, all of them, not separated by any class, all alone in their moments of reflection without any facade of falseness or subtlety, delicately loosening the tourniquet of their emotions, letting them bleed in their solitudes for just a moment, to cleanse themselves, before they wrapped them up tight again for another day.

It was the sadness of America being played by the man who probably understood it better than anybody else.

A genius, Gleason. There was nothing he couldn't do.

Joan must have caught just the end of the program, because the record ended and some colorless can of corn came on and started delivering a do-or-die spiel about the "gigantic advantage" of doing business at Joe Schlump's Appliance Store. "Gigantic and supercolossal and once in a lifetime . . . "

In disgust she reached across again and ripped the dial past half the stations on the air and then slowly began working her way back.

The noise of the crowd was what stopped her. The hollering and the shouting and the style of the band.

It was Guy Lombardo broadcasting from the Roosevelt Grill in New York over one of the networks . . . the Mickey Mouse music that everybody but the people had written off thirty years ago.

As Joan lay there listening to the gladness and the merriment she wondered if right now, at this very minute, there was anybody on the face of this very earth that was as miserable as she.

It was New Year's Eve, and no matter where she turned there was testimony that this was the season of rejoicing.

Her husband.

The radio.

The bells ringing out down the street from St. John's Church.

Everything . . . everywhere. Lighthearted and free . . . happy and gay.

It was only her. Only she had to be different.

The rest of the world was barreling in overdrive, and here she was, alone in her self-made confinement, a voluntary prisoner, feeling sorry for herself and thinking about suicide.

She tried to shut it out and concentrate on the music, but the more she tried the more it assailed her, until it reached the point where she thought she was going to bust.

She snapped off the radio and lay there in the darkness, twisting and turning, kicking her feet, pounding her pillow, and eventually starting to cry when none of it did any good.

After it was over she felt a little better and lay there perfectly still, inhaling deeply, trying to force herself to sleep. Her pillow was so clammy that she pushed it off on the floor and rested her cheek on the untouched freshness of the sheet.

Somewhere, after a period of time, she lost consciousness. As it is when you go to sleep, you never remember the exact moment. But she fell off and had the dream . . . the sensation of falling off the inevitable bridge in the inevitable nightmare that always hit her when she got sick.

The sensation of falling and of gasping for breath and of never hitting bottom and knowing that you can never return to the place from where you fell because when you did fall you broke through the black crepe into the other half of the world, and all the time you were falling, falling head over heels, falling senselessly patternlessly lower and lower until you got just so low and at last sliced through and then you were no longer low but on top, high, really high of this other world, and so you sink lower and lower, never hitting anything and never allowing anything to hit you because, after all, you're Joan Henry, a human being with a brain in a mind of intelligence and you can fall faster and avoid quicker any of the tentacles that want to grasp you because well, I might as well tell you, Joanie, that while you are falling you are actually dead and these things that reach out for you are the moon and the stars and the Devil and God and they want to make you a part of them by some beautiful form of perverted reincarnation.

When she woke up it was three o'clock in the morning and the depression had gone. She got out of bed, dressed quickly, and went out through the back of the house to the garage.

She backed the car out of the drive and drove carefully over the slippery streets down to the town.

She circled around the Loop once and parked the car on the east side of Scott a half-block past the Louis Joliet. Then she hurried back and went directly into the Marine Room of the hotel from the Clinton Street side.

Nobody noticed her and she stood just inside the door out of the light for just a second looking over the crowd.

Since a half hour or so after midnight the activity had been in a state of general decline.

Everybody who had made it a point to be indoors to hoot

in the New Year had either gone home or gone on to do his drinking and celebrating somewhere else. Consequently, at this time the room was only maybe a third filled, with people who had come early and endured.

With the exception of an occasional outburst, nobody had the strength for too much hoopla, and the climate of the room was flat, like a bottle of carbonated soda that had been shaken too much and had lost its life.

The physical appearance of the room itself suggested a scene five minutes or so after the manifestation of a minor earthquake.

In certain places there were two or three tables pushed together, leaving vast gaps of empty floor space where there was nothing. There were tables with six chairs huddled around, and there were tables with none.

There were tables that looked like a liquor showcase and tables so clean and devoid of debauchery that a person could kneel down and receive the Host.

There were empty bottles, half-filled bottles, and broken bottles, bottles on their bases and bottles on their sides. There were lipstick-tipped straws hanging limply out of lipsticked-tipped glasses, beer glasses, wineglasses, whiskey glasses, and vials.

There were noisemakers, hats, streamers, confetti, balloons, crepe, an odd glove and a package of Tums along with numerous extraneous trivia all scattered about as samples of indifferent and undenying caprice.

Joan had just about made up her mind to sit at the bar when she caught sight of Peggy Powers motioning to her from one of the dimly lit areas in the far corner of the room.

Joan picked her way through the debris to the spot and stopped just in front of the table.

"What's this?" she asked, nodding her head at the crowd. "Are they giving away money at dawn?"

"Yeah, Joliet's busting loose," said Peggy Powers. "Sit down and pour yourself a drink."

"No thanks," said Joan. "I'll just sit here and soak up the atmosphere. What happened to good-time Charlie there?"

She was looking at Johnny Powers, who was three or four feet to Peggy's left, slouched down on the car-type seat with his head twisted back at a crazy angle, his eyes half-open and his mouth wide open, belting out an occasional snore.

"Oh, him," said Peggy casually. "Nothing unusual. He started drinking before supper and—"

"What? Gasoline?"

"I wouldn't doubt it," deadpanned Peggy. "Said something about getting primed and he's been this way since eleven o'clock. I don't even know how he made it down here."

"Husbands, huh?"

"Yeah," said Peggy, glancing over at hers. "Any minute now I expect him to wake up and ask me how much time till midnight."

She turned back to Joan then, took a deep breath and thoughtfully regarded her as if actually seeing her for the very first time.

"Where's Spence?" she asked.

"At the Candlelight."

"Alone?"

"How should I know?"

"What happened? You two have a fight?"

"None of your business."

"Now, Joanie—"

"Well, it isn't, Peg. I don't ask you what goes on behind your bedroom door, do I?"

"I wouldn't tell you if you did."

"Well, there you are."

They sat there woodenly for just a moment after that, both of them staring down at the tablecloth in silence.

To alleviate the awkwardness Joan reached forward, singled out a clean glass, and poured herself a stiff shot of Carstairs and a negligible proportion of Seven-up. She raised it to the front of her face, held it there for just a second, and looked over at Peg.

"Happy New Year," she said.

Peggy smiled thinly, picked up her own half-filled glass, and reached over and clinked it with Joan's.

"Happy New Year," she said.

They just chatted aimlessly after that. Just sat there and talked about everything from the dry routine of their jobs at OAC to the unexpected excitement that the crazy Shirley Wilson had created last week when she had tried to kill herself by jumping into the canal from the Jefferson Street bridge.

It was altogether meaningless dialogue, not in the least constructive or destructive, just something to serve as a space filler between now and the time that they would leave.

As far as Joan Henry was concerned, the whole damn town could go jump into the canal from the Jefferson Street bridge . . . en masse. It wouldn't bother her a bit.

Peggy Powers didn't care either. She was worried about how she was going to drag her husband home in one piece.

She had been ready to leave hours ago, but when she saw Joan and motioned her over she felt she was obligated to sit there awhile and keep her company.

They must have sat there an hour or longer talking about nothing before they finally reached the saturation point. They started repeating themselves, and Peggy Powers just stopped talking and laughed, turned away from Joan, and reached over and started shaking her husband.

She had a very tough time with him for a while. Johnny Powers was grouchy and sleepy and disagreeable, and when he finally opened his eyes it was obvious that he didn't know where he was. Every time she had him upright in a sitting position and let go he would slip back down again, completely limp and useless.

As Peggy looked back at Joan and shrugged in hopeless futility she noticed that the last pair of couples in the room besides themselves were getting up preparing to leave. That settled it for her right there.

She reached over for her husband again, pulled him up by the hair, and shook his head. She slapped his face, jabbed him viciously in the ribs four or five times, and talked to him, telling him anything she could think of to arouse him and asking him repeatedly if he was awake and if he understood.

Johnny Powers just sat there absorbing it all without saying a word, like a football dummy being hit by the scrubs.

Peggy, who could be cruel when she made up her mind, just kept slugging him until she got him to the point where he could stand up and walk with her support. Then she looked back at Joan and asked her if she was ready.

Joan Henry herself wasn't crazy about going anywhere. As far as she was concerned, it felt like eight or nine o'clock, with the bigger part of the night still to be lived.

She had had an adequate rest and she didn't feel a bit tired. But there was everything else drawing up and withering away before her very eyes.

The good times had expired while she had been asleep, and now there was nothing left to do. She got up, put on her coat, and started walking out of the hotel ahead of Peggy and her husband.

When Joan Henry walked she walked very quickly and very impatiently, striding big, looking neither to the right nor to the left. It was an affected detachment she had acquired because she knew that wherever she went somebody was always staring at her and it made her too self-conscious.

Inside she was warm and tender and softhearted, but she hid it so well that ask anybody and nine out of ten would tell you that she was cold and indifferent. It was so much a part of her now, so habitual, that she walked this way whether there was anybody around or not.

The lobby of the Louis Joliet was empty, and it was only a few short strides from the Marine Room to the main exit. Appearing as the avant guard for the three, however, Joan Henry walked out like the place was on fire and stood just inside the front door looking out at the street waiting for Peg.

Peggy wasn't too far behind, but she was having a hard time with her husband, holding him with both hands around the upper part of the arm, trying to provide the moral courage to get him out to the street on his own.

As Johnny Powers walked out of the Marine Room he was weaving and lurching, but when he got outside into the lobby he suddenly seemed to become aware of himself and he jerked away in contempt of his dependence upon a woman.

He yanked himself sideways with such force that his feet got tangled and his momentum pirouetted him across the floor, where he fell flat on his face just short of the couch in front of the fireplace at the far side of the room.

Peggy walked over and grabbed him by the back of his collar as he was trying to struggle his way up and was starting to lead him away when she noticed the feet sticking out just beyond the edge of the couch.

She guided her husband into an armchair resting against the wall, where he went limp immediately. Then she went around to where the feet were and looked down at this man who was lying on his stomach with his head buried beneath a pillow.

At first she thought it was just another drunk who had passed out before he could make the street and she was just about ready to leave when the person turned himself over and exposed the whole of his face.

Peggy Powers stood frozen for just a moment and then

took two or three steps forward to make sure. Then she hurtled around and ran to the front door.

"Joanie," she said excitedly. "Joanie, come quick. Come quick. You wanna see something? You wanna get a kick? Come over here. Come on! Hurry up!"

"What? What are you talking about? See what?"

"Come here," persisted Peggy, pulling her by the sleeve. "Take a look at this!"

She pulled Joan back into the lobby and steered her to the position in front of the couch where she had stood after she had first seen the feet.

"Know who that is?"

Joan Henry just stood there staring down at that face without saying a word.

"Know who that is, Joanie? Remember him? Wally Janik? I read where somebody called him the greatest writer of our time. Remember him?"

Joan Henry just stood there staring down at that face without saying a word.

"Who'd have ever thought?" Peggy said. "Who would have ever imagined? Not in a million years. Never talked to anybody. Never went anywhere. I always thought he was such a baby. You knew him, didn't you, Joanie?"

"I knew who he was, but I didn't know him, no."

"I'll never forget," Peggy said. "I saw him this one time in Chicago at Marshall Field's autographing copies of his book. The crowd! You couldn't even get close. Now look at him."

"A real mess," said Joan Henry.

"Yes," Peggy said.

"A smelly, drunken bum."

Peggy Powers looked at her strangely.

"I thought it was him," said Peggy. "I thought I saw him in there drinking earlier in the night, but then I said no, what would he be doing back here . . . in Joliet . . . on New Year's Eve?"

Joan Henry just stood there staring down at that face without saying a word.

"Well," sighed Peggy, moving around and walking over to the chair where she had deposited her husband, "we're not getting rich doing this. C'mon, Bozo," she said, urging him to his feet once more, "we'll take you home and put you to bed and try it again next year. C'mon now."

Johnny Powers pushed himself up with an assist from his wife, and together they managed to navigate a wobbly path to the front door. Peggy was about to go out to the street when she turned around and saw Joan Henry still standing in that exact same spot in front of the couch.

"Joanie. Are you coming, Joanie? Joanie—"

Joan Henry just stood there staring down at the face without saying a word.

"C'mon, Joanie. You've seen him before. What is there to see?"

Joan Henry lingered just a second longer and then broke quickly away and walked out with Peggy to her station wagon. She then held open the door as Peggy jockeyed her husband into the seat, said goodnight and then hurried around the corner to her own car.

She got into the Studebaker, started it, flicked it in gear, and then gunned it furiously through the deserted streets that led back to the West Side.

Two or three minutes later, she skidded to a halt in front of her beautiful white house on Hickory Street.

She turned off the motor and sat perfectly still for a moment listening to the ebb tide of her own labored breath. There was no other car in front of the house or in the driveway, so apparently her husband was still out.

She got out of the car and started walking up the path to

the house when she suddenly changed her mind. She turned around and walked two blocks south into St. John's church.

She had a reason for not wanting to go into the house. There was no one there and she wasn't a bit sleepy or hungry and there would be nothing on the radio or television, so she just made up her mind and started walking the other way.

St. John's was really the very last place she ever thought she would find herself in at this time of night. She just looked up and there it was and it seemed like the most natural thing in the world to open the door and go inside.

Joan Henry couldn't remember when she had been here last. It was a place she passed twenty times a day and never gave a second thought to.

As she stood motionless in the vestibule for a minute, her first impulse was to turn around and walk back out.

Joan Henry believed in God, but that's as far as it went. Religion she could leave to the nuns. Confession was nobody's business but her own. She was no religious zealot walking the streets in the early hours of the dawn searching for a sign.

But the calmness that seized her in that brief moment as she looked from one end of the church to the other, studying its order and inner symmetry, was like an overpowering magnet that drew her further inside as if she had no will of her own.

She walked toward the front of the church and sat down on the end of one of the pews midway up the aisle.

The interior of the church seemed to have shrunk. But it was that way with everything. The return to something after a long absence always made it seem smaller.

All the frescoes and icons, the outraged martyrs drooping woundedly on crosses, the moon-faced madonnas with purity in their eyes, they all seemed so tragic and so real that she was unable to understand the paradox of insignificance and grandeur that they inspired in her.

Joan Henry sat in the emptiness of St. John's church for a long time that night thinking about everything that had ever happened in her life.

Her childhood.

Her girlhood.

Her marriage.

Everything.

She sat and she thought.

She sat and she thought.

Throughout the country the advent of day was like the flag signaling the end of a campaign. Those that had survived still went through the motions, but the sincerity was shot.

The bells had been rung, the wine had been drunk, the women had been loved, and the stories created to last the rest of the year.

As the light filtered through the windows of a small church on the West Side of Joliet, the most beautiful woman in the world got up from her pew and walked to the railing in front of the altar.

She wavered uncertainly for a moment, then blessed herself slowly and arched her body upward as she sank down to her knees.

"Dear Lord," she started to say, "my God . . . "

PART III

THE NEW YEAR

When Janik woke up it was all quiet and serene and whatever had been had expended itself in the night and died.

He pushed himself up into a sitting position, dropped his head down into his lap, and covered the sides of his temples with his hands. The stillness seemed cavernous, like sitting in an empty fight stadium long after the crowd had gone home.

He straightened up and looked around him.

The lobby was deserted. No one at the desk. No one in the Marine Room. No one up on the mezzanine. No one coming in or going out. If he only had a gun he could shoot up the place and run like a bastard and nobody would ever know.

He got up and walked out the front door into the street.

There were promises of dawn fighting for recognition in the east, and it had started to snow again. Not a heavy, persistent snow, but a light, immature drop that seemed to coincide with the earliness of the day.

Janik, the only person on the street, paced back and forth nervously in front of the hotel trying to make up his mind.

He was anxious to get the hell out of this town. He couldn't understand why in the hell he had ever come down here in the first place. On the other hand, he was hungry, and it would be a hell of a long train ride back to Chicago if he didn't eat.

He started walking in one direction, south, toward the station, stopped, came back, turned around in a complete circle, stepped off the curb, looked up and down the street, and then started walking forward again over the same imprints he had just backtracked.

There was only one possibility at this time of night . . . morning. Schnieter's . . . over on Chicago Street. If that wasn't open he would have to settle for a Coke and a bag of chips at the bar next door to hold him until he got back to Chicago.

At the end of Scott he swung west on Jefferson and headed up toward Chicago. Just as he reached the end of the corner he slowed down, playing it like a hardened card shark squeezing out the last hidden spade for a royal flush, and caught a glimpse of the spent neon sign in the window of the restaurant, flickering falteringly on the sidewalk.

It was all downhill as he picked up his step to the door.

When he got inside, he sat down at the second table from the front perpendicular to the wall. He was surprised to see that the waitress was still the old German girl, Millie, who had been here the first day he ever walked into the place.

Janik remembered her especially because he used to come in every night right after work for supper and she had always waited on him like a mother on a son, fussed over him and always asked him if everything was all right before she moved on to another customer.

When she finished waiting on a couple in evening clothes at the counter she came over to the table and he ordered two hamburgers, well, a double order of fries, and a large glass of milk.

Janik was more than a little disappointed when Millie just wrote it down and walked away like she had never seen him before and never expected to see him again.

Well . . . four years was a long time. She probably had a new favorite.

He shifted his chair and leaned back sloppily, stretching his legs under the table to a chair at the opposite side.

After a few minutes in this position he got tired and eased his legs off the chair, still leaving them extended a conspicuous distance past the opposite edge of the table.

When Millie brought his food he automatically straightened himself up and shoveled it down wolfishly, stopping only to motion her over for a second glass of milk.

After he finished eating, he loosened his belt, propped his legs back up on the chair, and leaned back to watch it snow and get light.

Even though there was no question now of the newness of the day, people were still dipping in and out of the bar next door, trying to prolong the night and the gladness, refusing to admit that it was over, wringing it for its last drop of goodness, like an aging gigolo who had exhausted himself gathering the graces of a prolific woman who had since grown weary of his services.

Right outside the restaurant, at the taxi stand, cabs were pulling in and out in an endless procession of one.

They were working like ambulances at a disaster location, slipping in, stopping momentarily, loading, and then departing . . .

Quietly . . .

Without hesitation . . .

Wasting no time . . .

Waiting for nothing . . .

It was an activity that wouldn't let up until noon, or sooner if the snow got too heavy.

Sitting there, looking at what was going on in the morning and thinking about what had transpired the night before, it suddenly occurred to Janik that if there was any one thing that would justify this trip, give any of it any meaning, it would be St. John's.

He wasn't an overly religious person. He didn't believe in God as a stock panacea to all his problems; but before, whenever things had gotten too tough and the loneliness had become unbearable he used to walk down the hill from Woodworth to Hickory and sit inside the church for as long as it took for the pressure to ease.

There was a certain peace in knowing that he was only a few blocks away from her house. A peace and a torture, too, because the temptation was always there to go and knock on her door and blurt out the whole thing, but nerve never allowed.

So he would sit there because it was quiet and he could get his thoughts straight and think of her and pray for her happiness, pray that she wasn't tortured by anyone the way she tortured him, and pray not to be hateful or bitter because she rejected him and he wanted her more than anything else in the world.

He would say it to himself and to the emptiness; to the remembered ones in the flickering candles and to the unemotional, straight-faced saints on all sides of him, including the heavily bearded old gentleman up on the ceiling crowned like the Statue of Liberty dressed in a loose, flowing sports robe that resisted his body like it had been passed off on him by a Maxwell Street shyster.

But that was silly. A long way in the past. The story of a young and lovesick kid alone in a strange town for the first time in his life with nobody to talk to and nowhere to turn.

St. John's had done a job for us, and we would always remember and be grateful.

But who in the hell needed religion when he had success?

Not all the success in the world, but enough so that he could afford to tell anybody to go to hell without thinking about it twice.

Who needed it?

No doubt about it, thought Janik, leaning back, coming back had been silly and he felt like a fool.

He could have spent New Year in Chicago on Rush Street and really had a ball. Tested the show at Mr. Kelly's or the Black Orchid, gone over to Oak Street and mingled with the characters at the Surfside or jostled all night with the gypsies just across the street at the Ranch. He had been asked to half a dozen parties in Hammond and Cal City, and he had thrown everything over just to come down here.

It was senseless.

An impetuous, crazy, senseless thing to do.

But then nothin' about this goddamn town ever made sense.

Never.

Not when he first came here . . .

Not when he worked here . . .

Not when he left here . . .

And certainly enough . . .

Least of all . . .

Not even now . . .

Years later . . .

When it was all over . . .

And he had no business here.

Janik got up, left a dollar for Millie, paid the check up in front to a fat counterman, and walked out again into Chicago Street. He crossed Chicago at the light and swung east on Jefferson back to the station.

As he worked his way past the Woodruff he noticed a few people sitting in the coffee shop, a handful at the counter and two or three couples vis-à-vis in booths, slouched down in various degrees of weakness.

They sat there, unmarked by time, lingering over a cup of coffee, discussing the night, lavishly enjoying the leisure that the morning afforded.

When he reached the east end of the Woodruff he turned the corner and hugged the building for twenty or thirty feet trying to keep out of the snow before he broke away and ran diagonally across Scott into the station. He made his way up the stairs to track level and walked up to the ticket office.

The agent was sitting there with his back to the window reading a paperbound edition of Bromfield's *The Rains Come.*

If he heard Janik tramping up the stairs or sensed he was standing there, he didn't show it because he paid no attention to him and went right on reading until he finished the bottom of the page.

Janik just stood there patiently and waited for him to get up.

He was just about to make some kind of sound when the agent sighed heavily, marked his place, and laid down the book. He laid it down reluctantly, as if hating to leave Fern Simon, alias Blythe Summerfield, the Pearl of the Orient, alone in a touchy situation.

"Yes, sir," he said, coming forward.

"One way to Darjeeling."

"Which line?"

"The GM& O?"

"Not today."

"The Santa Fe?"

"Nope."

"The Rock Island?"

"Hardly."

"But I gotta get home. India needs me."

"India needs a lotta things."

"I'll settle for Chicago."

"One-way?"

"One-way," nodded Janik.

The agent turned around, lifted a slide of yellow cardboard out of the rack, validated it, and flipped it over to Janik.

"Dollar fourteen," he said.

Janik had a pocketful of change, sort of a slush fund from all the drinking, and gave him the exact amount.

"Due in now, right?"

"He's late," said the agent. "You got about fifteen minutes."

"Which track?"

"The outside track. You'll have to walk up to the *Herald News* sign. All the way up."

"Right."

Janik went back and sat down on one of the benches facing the clock and watched the minutes click away with monotonous precision.

He looked around and noticed that there were two or three people well separated on the benches waiting for the same train. Probably conscientious insurance company bookkeepers or clerks who would be hunched over their desks and ready to go to work at the exact predesignated minute anything short of a tornado, the epitome of a tidal wave, or the sure-faced desolation of an atomic attack.

You never got to know people like that because you never saw their faces . . . only their backs.

A few more people straggled in during the next few minutes, each one covered with a light layer of snow.

There was a pretty girl, an ugly man, a station attendant, and a stoop-shouldered, mountainous old colored woman carrying a bulging shopping bag who went up to the agent to buy her ticket and then came back down and eased herself onto the bench five feet or so to Janik's left.

She was wearing an older coat of another time, battered and formless, with each of the buttons a different design and color; black hightops cracked with age, the kind that you laced criss-crossed into open-ended hooks and tied at the top; and a wrinkled white babushka imprinted with a purple map of Korea.

She sat down and unraveled her hand out of the bundle and rested a minute. Then she picked up her purse and took out a coin.

She came over in front of Janik to the scale, examined it momentarily, and then stepped up and put in her money.

The needle went up to fifty-two pounds and quit.

She shifted her weight a couple of times, banged the outside of the face with her fist, exhorted it harshly, implored it tenderly, all with no apparent result. Then she stepped down disgustedly and came away cursing in outraged blasphemy.

She came back to the bench and sat there for a minute or two thinking about it. Watching her, you could almost make book that she wasn't going to give it up at this.

She opened her purse again, took out another coin, pushed herself up, and reapproached the monster with the wariness and deference that a simple mind has for the complexities of something mechanical.

When she came astride it, however, her attitude suddenly changed and she kicked it a couple of times at the base, shook it, pounded the glass, and jabbed her finger in the coin return two or three times for good measure.

Thus satisfied, she stepped on once again, wet the penny in her mouth, and let it drop with an extra push into the machine.

She stood there holding her breath and watched the indicator rise up to fifty-two pounds and quit.

Not knowing what else to do short of turning the whole thing upside down, which she could have done very easily, she stepped down and came back to the bench, shaking her head vehemently and muttering in undisguised horror.

"Man," she was saying. "Man, man, man, man, man!"

Janik, watching her every move, was laughing so hard the had to get up and walk away.

He walked across the floor and stopped in front of the swinging doors leading out to the tracks.

He couldn't have been standing there more than a minute when the girl, the pretty one he had noticed walk in when he was sitting on the bench, came up and stood beside him.

At first she just stood there and looked blankly out at the snow. Then she turned and began staring openly at him.

At first Janik wasn't sure if she was staring at him or through him, but when she kept it up he gave her his attention and she smiled.

He was surprised to see that she was much prettier than her profile first indicated and much younger, too. Probably in her late teens or just out of them. In a couple of years it would be no exaggeration to call her beautiful. It was no exaggeration now.

Janik smiled at her and then turned his attention back to the window. The girl, however, did not let up and kept staring as forcefully as before.

Janik ignored it awhile and then turned back to her, but she cut him short.

"Pardon me," she said apologetically, "but aren't you Walter Janik? Mister Walter Janik? The writer?"

In the flash of half a second a dozen clever lines popped into Janik's head, but when he saw that the kid was dead serious he was compelled to play it straight.

"Yes," he said. "That's right."

"I read your book," blurted the girl. "I think you're the greatest."

"The greatest?" said Janik. "The very greatest? Of all time?"

"Yes," nodded the girl, "that's what I mean. Of all time."

"Well, that takes in a lot of territory," said Janik. "Who else have you read?"

"Oh, everybody," said the girl, "just everybody. Hemingway and Steinbeck and Joyce and Mann—"

"—and Sabatini and Veblen and Hardy and Spinoza."

"Well no," admitted the girl. "Not all those. But they can't be very important because I would have read them."

"Don't feel bad," said Janik. "I never read them either."

The girl laughed.

"Are you from Joliet?" asked Janik.

"Yes."

"I used to live here, you know. Maybe we know the same people."

"Give me a try."

"Oh, let's see," said Janik. "The Powers, the Fitzgeralds, the Oldhams, Russ Honrud."

"No," said the girl slowly, "I don't know any of them."

"They all live up on the West Side."

"Oh, I don't know anybody up on the West Side," said the girl. "I just know the plain people."

Janik laughed.

"What's your name?" he asked.

"Green," said the girl. "Marilyn Green."

"And you just know the plain people, huh?"

"That's right," said Marilyn. "Nobody important."

"You know me."

"I wish I did," said Marilyn. "Really well. Then I could force you to go out with me and make everybody jealous."

"You wouldn't have to push too hard, kid, lemme tell ya."

A faint whistle off in the distance, barely audible, made Marilyn look at her watch and frown.

"My train," she said. "It'll be here in a few minutes."

"I thought you were going to Chicago."

"No," said Marilyn. "I'm going south. To Dwight."

"Oh," said Janik. "Too bad."

"I know," said Marilyn Green. "Why is it you always meet somebody interesting when you only have five minutes?"

"I don't know," said Janik. "I really don't. That's just the way the kookie rumbles . . . every time."

"That's funny," she laughed. "You're funny."

"Yeah, I'm a clown," said Janik. "A real comedian."

At that particular moment the whistle in the distance erupted again with a series of punctuated blasts. It was louder now and closer and coming fast.

Marilyn Green took a yellow kerchief out of her pocket and folded it into a neat triangle. She draped it loosely around her head, pulled it back, pushed it up, and then half-knotted two corners of it under her chin.

"There," she said. "All set."

"Well, look," said Janik, glancing back over his shoulder, "we ain't got much time. Why don't you give me your number or tell me where you live? If I make it down this way again I'll give you a call."

"You mean it?" said Marilyn Green, taking him in narrowly. "You don't mean it," she said. "You're just a smooth operator playing out the string for a hick."

"No, wait—"

"No, it's all right," she said, holding him up. "You don't have to say the things that parting protocol demands. Not for me . . . I understand."

"No, you don't."

"Yes, I do," Marilyn said. "And it's all right. This is enough for me. Really it is. I'll remember it always."

"So will I," said Janik.

"No, you won't," Marilyn said. "There's no reason why you should. But it doesn't make any difference."

"I'll remember," assured Janik. "I'll write my next book just for you."

"Oh no," Marilyn said excitedly. "You mustn't! Don't do it! Don't ever write again!"

"What?"

"Don't ever write again," Marilyn said excitedly. "Don't ever write another book."

"Why?"

"Because you could never top it," said Marilyn Green. "Not in a hundred million years. Nobody could!"

"There have been great ones written before mine," said Janik kindly. "You're putting me up on a pedestal and that's the most dangerous thing you could ever do . . . with anybody."

"Well, I don't care," said Marilyn stubbornly. "Let them talk about their *War and Peace* and their *Scarlet Letter* and all their stuffy classics. Yours stand so far head and shoulders above anything else that's ever been written it's a shame. There's no comparison. It was perfect. I've read it so many times I could recite almost every page by heart.

"But don't ever write again," she pleaded. "Promise me you won't. After *High above the Earth* anything else would be a big comedown."

Janik took a good long look at her, at the urgency in her eyes, and then turned away and stared straight ahead out the window.

"I wish it was that simple," he said. "For whatever it's worth, I used to think that way myself once. Way back when I first started to write. One book and that's it, I said. A one-shot deal and it'll be the greatest. I'll make it that way. I'll make a bundle and then I'll quit.

"But you can't do it," he said, turning back to her. "They won't let you. Make it big today and you're no longer a name; you're a property. All of a sudden there are other considerations. They cut you up into so many pieces. You get used to a certain mode of life. Everything changes. So you see it's not as simple as it all sounds, even though you're a hundred percent right."

"Well, it's your story," said Marilyn. "You do what you have to. I guess I'm too naive anyway. Too much of an idealist. Too Joliet. Whatever you wanna call it.

"With me life is a good man, a roof over my head, and a couple of kids. That's as much as I would ever want. Listening to you it's all circles within squares within rectangles within trapezoids. Big business."

The sound of escaping steam and the singsong of a bell suddenly echoed with collision volume and broke the thread of understanding between them.

Marilyn moved to one side of the door to get a better look out the window and just managed to catch a glimpse of the leading edge of the locomotive easing its way along the straightaway into the station proper.

"Well, this is me," she said, looking reluctantly. "Good-bye, Mr. Janik."

"Good-bye, Miss Green."

"You'll remember?"

"I'll remember."

"You promise?"

"I promise."

Janik pushed open the door for her, and the girl brushed past him with a proximity that jumped him inside.

She took two or three quick steps toward the platform, hesitated, stopped completely, and then pivoted abruptly in her tracks.

"Imagine," she said incredulously. "Right here in Joliet. Nobody will ever believe me."

Then she wheeled around and zigzagged her way through the spots where the snow was lightest to the train.

After she got on, Janik looked for her, searched each

window thinking perhaps she would wave or smile, make some sign of final farewell, before the train pulled out.

He searched from where she had boarded to the right as far as he could discern faces and was on his way back over the same distance when, without warning, the wheels of the locomotive suddenly spun and caught, the rest of the cars' chain reacted accordingly, and the 6:01 to Manteno disappeared in growing miniature around the bend.

For a minute or two after the train was gone Janik stood in the snow outside the door, staring blankly out toward the general area where it had last passed from view.

Within himself he felt hollow and empty and cheated, just like some subtle con artist had drained the last drop of blood out of his veins in a nefarious swindle.

What was the answer? he thought.

He had to be off somewhere to feel like this. Starting from the beginning and working it up to the present, the whole thing just had to be wrong. It had to be.

But then how could he have done anything differently?

Just how?

If he took it apart piece by piece, objectively and without emotion, he could show anybody that he was right.

You make up your mind when you're young where your talent is and you develop it and if it kills everything else, well, that's the way is. You got a drive and you know what you want.

If you're any good at all you're a fatalist and if you're the greatest you're impossible, which is nothing new, because that's the way it's always been in anything.

So you work like a slave for years and pile up a satisfactory wall of material justification only to see it crumble every so often during one five-minute conversation with a kid.

Then as the air clears and the particles settle, somewhere off in right center the middle E lights up on the scoreboard to inform you without any question that life, that most uncompromising of all official scorers, has once again faulted you for your talent.

So as you stand there in your bewilderment you're like the guy that's caught between two worlds, one dead and one powerless to be born.

You're right, but you're wrong; you've created, but you've destroyed; you're everything, but you're nothing.

Go figure it.

Inside the station the loudspeaker barked a garbled announcement. It came on so unexpectedly and was repeated so quickly that the most Janik could catch was "to Chicago."

He straightened up and looked to the south, listening for some telltale sound that would give him an idea of the position of the train.

Despite the fact that he heard nothing, he left the protection of the overhang and started walking deliberately up-station.

From out of nowhere the wind had suddenly picked up, and it was starting to swirl the snow around in eddies.

Vicious eddies . . .

Consuming eddies . . .

Eddies with a mind.

Every time one of them blew up in Janik's face he turned his head to the side or buried it inside his overcoat and closed his eyes.

The last winter he had spent here had been like this. Bitter and severe and unyielding. The passage of four years hadn't changed it a bit.

And what about the people? What about them? Where were they? How had time treated them?

How many were still here?

How many had fled?

How many were successful?

How many had failed?

How many were happy . . .

And how many weren't?

Each one of them stood up and paraded before him in kaleidoscopic review just like the faces of the dead briefly flashing across the screen in retrospect just once more at the end of an old Foreign Legion film.

When he reached the *Herald News* sign he stopped and stood there on the open platform, shivering, bareheaded, remote, indifferent to everything but how he could start it when he got back to Chicago.

There was a fabulous story in it somewhere, he was thinking.

There had to be.